If I Can Do This Again

A Thomas Hall Novella

Beth Sorensen

In Memory Of

my beloved aunt, Betty Newsome.

She was always the first to ask about my current work in progress

and encouraged me to never give up.

One

I ROLLED OVER AS I woke, and the sunlight from the windows highlighted the empty pillow where Edward's head should be. I had been doing this for nearly three years. I knew he would never be there again, but every morning, before I opened my eyes, I prayed his death had been a nightmare. That I would find him lying there, with his big cocoa-colored eyes staring back at me.

I slipped on a warm robe before heading to the kitchen. It was cold and eerily quiet.

We moved into the house just days before Faith's arrival, but all three girls were grown now, and I often felt like I was rattling around in the massive square footage.

Edward and I designed it together, taking things we loved and incorporating them into the perfect place to raise children. If it weren't on the winery's property, I would have sold the house after Joy, our youngest, graduated from high school. However, it was one of the Thomas Hall Estate houses. And Hope, the oldest of our children, still lived at home with me.

Edward would always put on soft jazz and, this time of year, would light a fire in the fireplace. He did this most mornings during the winter, and February of this particular year seemed colder than usual.

More often than not, we'd dance for a couple of minutes while we waited on the toaster. The girls thought it was sweet when they were little and often cut in for a dance with their daddy, but when they were teenagers, it embarrassed them to no end.

Closing my eyes, I could almost feel Edward's hands on my waist, swaying me to the music.

My phone pinged as a flood of memories washed over me. It was Hope.

Hope: Would you have time to bring me my wallet?
I left it on my dresser. I'm having one of those days.

Of course. I'll be in town for Mass this morning.
I'll drop by the brewing company afterward.
If you need money before then, hit up your uncle.

Hope attended college long enough to get an associate's degree in brewing management and went to work for my brother-in-law, Henry Baker.

Everyone was happy with the arrangement except Edward. He wanted her at the winery with me. I reminded him that you couldn't choose your children's paths. Although he accepted it and was happy that she was happy, he knew it would not be her forever career.

Henry's kids would inherit the brewery, so Edward taught her everything he knew about commercial real estate. He wanted to ensure she had a second career to fall back on.

She was smart, savvy, and quickly amassing a fortune of her own. She was an amazing girl, even if she was a little absent-minded, disorganized, and had a habit of leaving her wallet on her dresser.

When I walked into the offices at The Baker's Dozen Brewing Company, I waved to the receptionist, Paige, as she spoke on the phone.

She was a sweet girl in her late twenties or early thirties. I knew little about her since she wasn't raised in the area. The classic blonde-haired, blue-eyed girl from California came to Virginia, looking for a fresh start. Because I understood needing a fresh start, I didn't ask too many questions.

I continued back to Hope's office. I had not been to the brewery since New Year's Eve. As always, the distinct aroma of the malt and yeast from freshly brewed beer filled my head. When I tapped on the door to her office, then opened it, she was sitting, speaking with a ginger-haired, bearded gentleman with a few tattoos peeking from the edge of his sleeves.

Something about the ginger hair, beard, and tattooed muscles made my mouth water. Frozen in the doorway, I found it alarming and bit my bottom lip. I hadn't responded that way to a man since before the death of my husband.

Hope waved me in, and I moved slowly. When I reached her desk, I fished her wallet out of my purse and handed it to her.

"Thanks, Mom."

Every time she looked at me, I saw her father's big cocoa-brown eyes. Hers had the same glittery shine when she flashed Edward's Cheshire cat grin at me.

"Anytime."

"Wait," the gentleman said with a heavy Irish accent. "This is your mum?"

"That's right. Y'all haven't met. Mom, I'd like you to meet Colin McAllister, our new brewmaster. Colin, this is my mother, Cassandra Baker."

He stood, and I smiled, shaking his warm, strong hand. He was the tallest man I had ever met. Easily six-foot-five. At some point, his hair was bright ginger but had since faded and mixed with silver. My guess was he was in his late fifties, maybe sixty. He was in great shape, and his muscular arms stretched the edges of his shirt's short sleeves.

"Hope, your uncle was right. Your mother is quite a beauty."

My brother-in-law had told me a little about the new brewmaster who started working for him at the beginning of January. The two men had become friends over the last month and a half and often met at the diner before starting their workday.

"You're too kind, Mr. McAllister."

Warmth rushed to my face, and I was certain it was red as I looked over to Hope. "I won't keep you. You look busy."

Hope walked around her desk and hugged me. She patted me on the head, like she always did when she was done. Hope was four inches taller than me and liked to remind me of it.

"Before I forget, I won't be home for dinner tonight. I have a date with Mark."

"That's the third one in the last two weeks," I said. "Sounds like it might be serious."

She shrugged. "Not really. Are you going to be okay alone tonight?"

"Of course. Maybe I'll pick up Italian to take home." As the words came out of my mouth, I had a thought. "Mr. McAllister, would you and your family like to join me for dinner tonight? The Italian restaurant in town is excellent."

"First, the name's Colin. Second, I'm single, and third, my children live in Dublin, but I'd love to join you."

"Oh, I assumed you had a family."

"Not in The States. But dinner out does sound good."

"Great, text me when you're done with work for the day." I pulled a Post-it note from Hope's desk and wrote down my cell number.

Hope raised an eyebrow and looked at me as I turned to walk out of her office. Even her expressions reminded me of her dad. It wasn't until I was out the door and on the sidewalk as the winter wind stung my face did I understand why Hope gave me that particular look.

"Oh my God," I said aloud to myself.

I had accidentally asked Colin McAllister on a date.

All the way back to the winery, I thought about it. I parked in front of the main house at Thomas Hall, where my mother-in-law, Vivian, lived. She was so much more than a mother-in-law. She was my friend, advisor, and surrogate mother.

I rushed into the warm house from the chilly February air and found Vivian in the library reading an old book. I dropped myself on the leather sofa next to her. She said nothing but gave me a look I had never seen from her as she closed her book and placed it on a side table.

"What happened? You look like you want to jump off a cliff."

"I think I already did."

"Tell me, what's going on?"

"I think I just asked the new brewmaster at The Baker's Dozen on a date tonight."

"That's great!"

She was quick to respond. Although I was married to her late son, she encouraged me to start dating again after the first anniversary of Edward's death.

So far, I chose not to seek companionship and politely declined dinner date requests.

"I. Should. Cancel."

Each word fell from my lips between shallow breaths.

"Cassandra, breathe. You're starting to hyperventilate."

I took a moment to catch my breath.

"I don't know what happened. One minute I was dropping off Hope's wallet, and the next minute, I was giving this man my phone number."

"This is good. You're too young to be a widow. You were the first time, too. You're not even fifty yet."

I stared at Vivian as my eyes filled up with tears.

"What is it, dear?"

"What would Edward think?"

I whispered my question, and a tear escaped. I wiped it away with the back of my hand.

"He wouldn't want you to be as lonely as you've been since he passed away. He would want you to be happy."

My phone pinged.

Colin: Hi! This is Colin McAllister.
Henry says tonight sounds like a date.
Is it?

I stared at my phone and bit my lip as I typed out a reply.

I don't know. I've not dated much.
Do you want it to be?

His response was quick.

Colin: Yes.

I will pick you up at your house at 7.

I showed the text to Vivian. As she held my phone, she typed but did not press send before handing it back.

Great.

I'll let the guard at the gatehouse know you're coming.

See you then.

"I saved the number to your contacts as well."

"I should cancel."

"No, you should press send. It's time."

I whole-heartedly disagreed with her, but I hit send anyway.

Two

THE DOORBELL RANG PROMPTLY at seven o'clock. When I opened the door, there, he stood, holding a bouquet. He was freshly showered in khaki pants and a blue button-down collar shirt with a black leather jacket.

"Wow, you look beautiful," Colin said.

My burgundy sweater dress fit my body perfectly without being so tight that it looked trashy. I paired it with black leather dress boots and left my hair down.

"Thanks. Come on in."

I realized after I spoke that I did not sound happy to see him. As he walked past me, I inhaled his cologne. Leather and vanilla invaded my senses and overtook my thoughts to where I almost missed what he said.

"Well, that's the least enthusiastic invitation I've heard in a while. Usually, a woman has to go out with me on two or three dates before I get that kind of reaction."

I smiled and quietly laughed under my breath. "Sorry. This is just weird for me."

He handed me the flowers, and I immediately thought of my late husband. He always made sure there were fresh flowers in the house for me. There had not been flowers in the house since his funeral. I requested that they no longer be placed in the house when cleaned. The reminder was more than I could bear when I first became a widow.

I turned away as I spoke, so he didn't see my teary eyes. "Thank you. I should put these in water before we go." I headed toward the kitchen, and he followed.

"You said this is weird for you. Why?"

"It's the first time I've been on a date since my husband died."

"Oh." I could tell he didn't know what to do with this piece of information, so he moved on. "This kitchen is amazin'."

"Edward designed it. He was a gourmet cook, among other things." I turned and faced Colin. "I'm sorry. I guess I shouldn't be talking about him with you. It's just that our lives were so very intertwined."

"As it should be," he said, gently resting a hand on my arm for a moment. The gesture was warm and caring. "Accordin' to Hope, the two of you had a love story for the ages. I thought she was exaggeratin', but now that I'm here and lookin' at all the pictures in your house, I can tell it's true."

I looked around, and there were dozens of pictures of us together, as a couple and as a family. At some point, the entire house had become a shrine, proclaiming the devotion Edward and I felt for our family and for each other.

"You could call the whole thing off, and I wouldn't think any less of you," I quietly said.

"Somehow, I believe that. However, you're in the mood for Italian food, and I'm hungry. So, let's go get some dinner."

We sat in a corner booth of the restaurant where we weren't visible to most of the other patrons at Casa de Mimmo's.

It was the quintessential Italian restaurant, with dim lighting, red checkered tablecloths, and candles on each table with wax dripping down the sides of empty chianti bottles. The owner was always kind and tried to keep my presence discreet. Over the years, the press stopped hounding me, and after Edward died, they left me alone.

Colin and I had our drinks in hand as the waitress took our order. The lack of conversation was unnerving for me, but he seemed comfortable enjoying his beer. I tried to focus on the Italian music playing in the background but kept getting pulled into my head, trying to come to terms with my being on a date with a man other than my husband. After a short battle, I was able to clear that thought from my head. At least for a while.

I was about halfway through my glass of wine when he struck up a conversation.

"Cassandra, if you don' mind me askin', how old are you?"

"I don't mind. I'm forty-eight. What about you?"

"I'll be sixty in a couple of months." He paused, waiting for a reaction from me. I think he expected me to be shocked that he was so much older than me. "You are much younger than I expected. Honestly, I just thought you had a great plastic surgeon."

"Thanks. It's funny, though. Forty-eight doesn't feel young."

I decided not to tell him about my regular Botox appointments.

"I imagine losin' a spouse so young can make you feel that way. Hope said her father died of a heart attack. Maybe that's why I thought you'd be older."

"Edward was sixty-eight when he died." I could almost see him doing the math in his head. "I'll save you the calculating. There was a twenty-two-year age gap between us."

"He was a lucky man. You knew you'd outlive him but chose to share your life with him anyway."

"Have you ever been married?" I asked.

"No. I wanted to marry the woman who is the mother of my children, but she didn' want to. One of my many regrets was not pushin' her more to marry me. We ended our relationship when the boys were thirteen and sixteen. Less than a year later, she married an accountant from Dublin and moved the kids there." Sadness laced his eyes and voice. "But that was years ago. The boys are grown now. Hope's not your only child. Tell me about the others."

"Hope's the oldest. You know about her. Next is Faith. She's a year younger and is at Appalachian State studying fermentation science. She'll graduate in December and come work with me and

Alex at Thomas Hall Winery. My youngest is Joy. She's two years younger than Hope and at Georgetown in their pre-law program. Her current plan is to work for the company her father was CEO of, Chesapeake Biotech."

"Wait a minute. Three girls in three years?"

"Yeah. All born in December. Edward wasn't young when we started, and I wanted a big family. We had to stop at three, though. I had some health issues while giving birth to Joy."

"How many more would you have had if the circumstances were different?"

"Oh, at least a couple more. But things worked out the way they were supposed to," I said with a smile.

"On the surface, it looks like you've had a beautiful life, but I have a feeling there is more below the surface that's not as great."

"There is, but I try not to focus on the bad. You can't change the past. You can only move forward."

Three

BY THE TIME HE pulled his truck up to the front of my house, I had wrapped a few strands around my finger so tightly that it cut off the circulation at the tip of my index finger. Colin looked straight ahead as he killed the engine, and we sat in the cold, dark interior of his truck for a full minute before anyone spoke.

"Want to know a secret?" Colin asked.

"Sure."

"This is the first date I've been on in over a year."

"No? Really? You made it look easy. Like you do this all the time."

The conversation was awkward for me but got easier as the night went on. He was great at entertaining me with stories of his life and asking questions without intruding on my privacy.

He turned to me and smiled. It was small and simple. No teeth showing, no ear-to-ear grin. Just a simple smile.

"I'd like to do this again if you're interested."

"I think I'd like that." I untwisted the hair from my finger, leaned over, and kissed him on the cheek. The whiskers from his soft beard tickled my skin. As soon as I did it, I wondered if it was the right move. "Good night, Colin."

I walked in the door to find Hope sitting in the living room with a scowl.

"How was your date?" I asked, taking off my coat and boots.

"Terrible."

My phone pinged, and I glanced at it.

Faith: Danger, Will Robinson

Faith had watched too many episodes of *Lost in Space* as a child. However, I knew what she meant.

Hope was about to go on a tirade. She was quick to anger and had a history of leaving a trail of bad decisions and hurt feelings when she was in this state.

Hope slid away from me when I sat on the sofa.

"What happened? I thought things were going well with Mark."

"Well, not anymore. And it's your fault."

"I'm confused. Would you like to explain?"

"Sure," she said. "We were at the bowling alley, and we had just finished our first game. The waitress that delivered our pizza looked me straight in the face and asked me if it was going to be weird being my new daddy's boss."

"New daddy? That's where the gossip is going? What is that supposed to mean, anyway?" I asked, even though I knew what the waitress was implying.

I hated that anyone thought Edward could be replaced.

"Mom, everybody in town is talking about you and Colin dating!"

"Hope, you know how the gossip is in town. We aren't dating. It was one dinner. He moved to town a couple of months ago. You were there this morning. I was just being polite."

"Are you going to see him again?" Hope asked.

"Possibly. He's good company. How would you feel about that?"

"Here's a taste of how I'd feel about it. I yelled at the waitress tonight until she cried and then yelled at her manager. Mark was trying to calm me down and convince me we should head out. So, I yelled at him, too. Then I left. I got in my car and drove home."

Tears ran down her face while she spoke. There was more to this. And I knew what it was.

"Hope, just say it."

"How could you do this to Dad?!"

I took a deep breath. "I've asked myself that question a dozen times today. I even talked to your grandmother about it. She reminded me I wasn't doing anything to him, and he'd want me to find someone to be happy with."

"You don't know that."

I sighed. The problem with Hope was that she always thought she knew more than she did.

"Actually, I do. After your dad's second heart attack, he sat me down one night when the three of you were at summer camp, poured me a glass of wine, and told me what he wanted me to do when he died. The doctors told us he probably wouldn't survive another heart attack. It was the hardest conversation we ever had, and we had a lot of hard ones during our marriage. Your dad held me, and I cried all the way through it. We talked about what he wanted his funeral to look like." I swallowed hard, reliving that night in my mind. "He told me how he wanted me to tell each of you certain things at certain points in your lives, and just when I thought he was done, he told me I would be too young to stay a widow. I should find someone to spend the rest of my life with. To be happy and remarry. I told him I would remarry when hell froze over."

Hope wiped the tears from her face and stared at me. It was as if—possibly, for the first time—she realized this was not about her or her sisters. It was about what her father wanted for me.

"God, Mom"—she reached over and squeezed me in a hug—"sometimes, I forget y'all knew this was coming. I understand why you didn't want to worry us about the possibility that Dad could die when we were all so young. Dad was right, though. You're too young to be a widow. I just don't know how to handle you dating."

Before the girls were born, I decided not to tell our kids about my abusive first husband. There was always the possibility of them stumbling upon the information, but, somehow, they didn't find out. I knew it was time.

"I was too young to be a widow the first time, too."

"Wait? What? What do you mean?"

"Someday, I'll tell you the whole story, but your father was not my first husband."

Within the hour, I was in my favorite nightgown, and my phone was blowing up. First, it was Zoe Marshall. She was my dearest girl-friend, the common-law wife of my brother-in-law, Henry Baker, and the owner of Zoe's Day Spa & Boutique.

Zoe: I heard you had a big date with a ginger-haired hottie!

It was dinner. That's all.

Zoe: Are you going to go out again?

Maybe.

Zoe: Lunch tomorrow?

Sure. I'll come by the shop around noon.

Over the past few years, I slowly handed more of my responsi-bilities at the winery to my nephew, Noah Foster.

The plan was for him to take over my role as COO, and Faith would apprentice with—and eventually replace—Alex White, my brother-in-law, as winemaster when he was ready to retire.

A couple of days a week, I would pop in to work. One would say I was semi-retired, although I worked full-time during the harvest and bottling seasons. This left me with plenty of time to do as I pleased, including weekly lunches with Zoe.

Next was Joy.

Joy: Heard you went on a date tonight.
How did that go?

It was weird.
But it was nice to spend time with someone new.

Joy: Why weird?

I still love your dad.
I always will.

Joy: I know. It's okay.
I didn't know you were married before Dad.

I think it's time for y'all to know everything.
The next time we are all together, I'll tell y'all the whole story.

Joy: Is Hope still losing her mind?

A little.
Faith sent me a "Danger, Will Robinson" text.
It was a few seconds too late.

Joy: LOL!

When Faith hadn't sent another text by ten-thirty, I dropped one to her.

Thanks for the warning earlier.
It was about thirty seconds too late.

Faith: Sorry. How was it?

How was what?

Faith: The date!

Weird.
The whole thing felt weird.

Faith: I bet. I'm proud of you.
That had to be hard.

It was. But Colin's nice.

Faith: I'm glad.
You should go out with him again then.

I'm sure one of your sisters texted you about
Dad not being my first husband.

Faith: I've known since I was thirteen.
Uncle Alex let it slip once. I was sworn to secrecy.
Then I went home and Googled you.

After considering it, I thought Colin might enjoy hearing about the post-date conversation I had with my girls, so I dropped him a text.

My girls have had a lot to say about our dinner.

Colin: Good, I hope.

Hope got a little unhinged.
Joy, as usual, was cool with it.
Faith told me I should go out with you again.

Colin: I like Faith already.

She's my quiet one.
The fact she commented at all is impressive.

Colin: Hope went a little crazy?

All of my girls were Daddy's girls, but she was the closest to him.
She's the most protective of his memory.

Colin: Should I talk to her?

That's up to you.
I'm okay with it.
But I can't tell you whether or not it is a good idea.

Colin: I'll let you know if I do.

Henry's wife texted me too.
Prepare for an interrogation from Henry.

Colin: He just texted me.
We're meeting for breakfast at the diner in the morning.

I'm sorry.
I didn't even think of the fallout our dinner would cause.

Colin: You mean our date.

Four

A COLD WIND BLEW around stray, dried grape leaves as I walked in the sun to the production building. Last night's outing with Colin still occupied my mind. How mild-mannered he was for someone who, at first glance, appeared to be rough and intimidating was surprising. The man was a giant, a walking wall with muscular arms, a deep voice, piercing eyes, and a gentle soul.

My mind was still on Colin when Brian Hayes walked into my office about thirty minutes after my arrival. He had a chai latte in his hand for me and placed it on the desk before he sat with his own drink.

Brian and I met soon after I arrived at Thomas Hall.

He was a detective for the Willow Creek Police Department when we first met. Over the years, he climbed the ranks and was now in charge of law enforcement in Willow Creek.

He and my husband had a sordid past involving Brian's ex-wife, Stefanie Hayes. She was serving multiple life sentences for murder, among other things.

"Well, isn't this a role reversal?" I asked with a smile.

Usually, it was me walking into his office at the police station with a drink for him.

"Cassandra, how could you?"

Only when he asked the question did I look directly at him and notice he wasn't smiling.

"How could I what?"

"You know," he said, looking angry. "You've known how I've felt about you all of these years, and you go out with that tatted-up brewmaster instead?"

"Hold up a minute!"

My jaw dropped, and I took a moment to compose myself before continuing.

"I know you only took an interest in me all those years ago to get back at Edward and because I looked like your ex-wife. We have never been more than friends, and you never gave me any reason to believe that it was something you truly wanted."

"Then, go out with me tonight," he said, almost pleading.

"No."

"Why? Do you have plans with *him* again?"

"Not that it's any of your business, but no. I'm not sure if that will happen." I was hoping this would calm his emotions. "Hope's not handling it well. And his name is Colin."

"Yeah, I know. Colin McAllister. I looked into him. Looks like he did a couple of stents in juvie back in Ireland as a teenager. One was theft, and the other was drug related."

"And how old was he then?"

"Fifteen the first time. Seventeen the second."

"So, forty-five years ago. You are really going to hold something a sixty-year-old man did as a kid against him?"

Brian said nothing but sat and took a gulp of his drink.

Contemplating this situation, I sipped mine before moving away from Colin's past.

"Brian, we've been friends for over twenty years. Why is that suddenly not enough? Is it because someone else has my attention?"

This conversation was unexpected. Maybe I was wrong, thinking I knew Brian well.

"We may have been friends, but I've always wanted you." He stared into my eyes as he spoke.

"No," I said, shaking my head in disbelief. "If that were the case, I wouldn't have watched dozens of women fall into and out of your bed over the years. I've seen this behavior from you before. The only thing you ever want is the one thing you can never have."

"Well," Brian said sheepishly, "a guy still has needs, even if he's waiting."

"You sound like a sex-crazed teenager." I sighed. "I think you know I love you, but I'll never love you as anything more than a friend. I hope you can accept that."

"I don't know if I can. I need to think about this." He stood to leave, and when he got to the door, he turned. "I just need time. I thought I might stand a chance to be with you after Edward died. I didn't think you'd meet someone new and things would take off so fast."

"It's not that fast. And even if it was, it wouldn't change this conversation."

"You need to give me a chance. I've waited a long time for you to be single."

"Are you telling me you waited twenty years for Edward to die so you could get together with me?"

I must have looked as dumbfounded as I sounded.

"I would be lying if I said no."

"You're acting like I'm pursuing you. Not the other way around." I watched as he turned and walked away, not even saying goodbye.

If someone knew this would be the fallout from one dinner, I wish they would have told me.

"This is so messed up," I said to myself, shaking my head.

The morning flew by as I tackled a mountain of paperwork. Noah and I were going to have to talk about this. He avoided the government forms and license renewals necessary to keep Thomas Hall Winery operational. It was time to take a couple of hours once a week and sit together so he could learn what he needed to take over this responsibility.

As I hopped into my car to head into town for lunch with Zoe, my phone rang. I looked at the caller ID on my car's navigation screen before answering it with my vehicle's hands-free device.

"Good morning, Vivian."

"I'm angry with you," she said.

By the tone of her voice, I knew she wasn't.

"Uh-oh. What did I do today?" I asked with a smile on my face.

"You didn't call to tell me about your date. I want details. Where did you go? What did you do? Did he kiss you? Did he spend the night at your house? Let's be real here. It's been a while since you've—"

"Vivian! No, he most certainly did not spend the night. It was the first time we went out."

Vivian took a moment to control her laughter at my indignant but comical tone. "Cassandra, seriously, though. Did you enjoy yourself?"

"Yes, but it was weird."

"Weird how?"

"I'm not sure I can explain it. It wasn't Colin. He was wonderful. Kind, sweet, and great at keeping the conversation going. He asked lots of questions but not in a nosy way. He just wanted to get to know me."

"But?"

"But I felt like I had been dropped into an alternate universe. Sitting across the table on a date with a man that wasn't Edward felt foreign. I'm not sure I'll ever get used to that."

"And?"

I knew what she was asking.

"I gave him a kiss on the cheek at the end of the night after he asked me out again. That's all."

"It sounds like a nice place to begin," Vivian said. "Would you like to meet me and my sisters for lunch at the country club?"

"I'd love to, but I promised Zoe that I would meet her for lunch. Maybe next time."

Five

WHEN I WALKED INTO Zoe's Boutique, which was attached to her salon, it was busier than usual. I loved her place. A client could get a manicure, a pedicure, a hair and makeup revamp, and a new outfit all in one location.

Zoe was working the register and trying to assist customers. I walked behind the counter, put my purse underneath, and took off my coat. Once it was folded and placed on top of my bag, I hip-bumped Zoe out of the way so I could ring up customers. Twenty minutes later, just as the crowd cleared out, Henry and Colin walked in. I looked at them and then at Zoe.

"We were going to see if you wanted to join us for a late lunch. Sis, I didn't know you would be here."

Henry was a terrible actor and a worse liar.

"Zoe and I were supposed to have lunch, but it was Bedlam in here when I showed up."

"Nora no-showed again. I don't want to do it, but I'm going to have to let her go. I need dependable people working for me. I don't care that she's our niece."

As Zoe spoke, Colin made his way to me. He walked behind the counter, put an arm loosely around my waist, and kissed my temple.

He was such a sweet man.

"Do what you've got to do," Henry said. "Give Phoebe a heads-up, though. If you don't, my sister will get a different story from Nora, and I'll get yelled at."

"I guess that means no lunch today, then," I half said, half asked.

"Hell no. I'm closing the dress shop."

After the twins were born, Zoe changed the way the day spa operated. Before then, everyone working there was on Zoe's payroll. Now, they each rented their own space from her. This allowed the day spa to run without her.

"The four of us are going to lunch."

"Pelican Room?" I asked her.

"What the hell is the Pelican Room?" Colin asked.

"Get ready. We're going to the country club," Henry answered before looking at me. "Are you sure you want to walk into the lion's den?"

"Why not? According to Hope, the whole town is already talking. And ever since your mom mentioned the country club this morning, it's all I've been able to think about."

Colin looked at Zoe. "What am I missin' here?"

She laughed before answering him. "You've never lived in a small town before, have you? The gossip about you and Cassandra is about to blow up."

The country club went silent as we were taken to our table. The Pelican Room was more casual than the other dining areas at the club, so the guys were fine in jeans and sweaters. I had on black slacks and a purple cashmere sweater. Of course, Zoe looked fashionable, as always. The nature of her business required her to dress to impress daily.

Even once we were seated, no one else in the room spoke.

"Okay, I'll say it. This was a bad idea on my part. If y'all want to go someplace else, we can."

Colin was the first to speak up.

"If this is where you want to eat, then this is where we eat."

The waitress made her way to the table, and everyone ordered drinks after she rattled off the specials. I had not touched the menu when the waitress returned. Everyone else ordered, and when the waitress turned to me, she asked if I wanted my usual.

I nodded and smiled.

"You always order the same thing?" Colin asked.

"At lunchtime, she does," Zoe said. "Monte Cristo sandwich with no turkey, add deli-sliced chicken, and she always wants melon instead of onion rings."

Colin smiled. "A woman that knows what she likes."

My phone pinged. When I flipped it over, I saw it was from Vivian.

Vivian: Whoa! He's nothing like I expected him to look. Very hot!

Shaking my head, I glanced around in search of her. It only took a moment to find her and her sisters. I smiled and shook my head again.

"Who was it?" Henry asked.

"Your mother."

"Should I even ask?"

"You don't want to. Trust me." I turned to Colin. "Even as she approaches ninety, Vivian is very opinionated and not afraid to express those opinions."

"Hopefully, in a kind way."

My hand was sitting on the table, and he reached out, patted it, then gently held it in his giant hand. When he did, the room filled with the buzz of whispers.

"Absolutely, at least where you are concerned." I used my free hand to pass him my phone and then watched as his cheeks turned pink when he smiled.

The food arrived quickly, and I was thankful. It was uncomfortable sitting at a table with my late husband's brother and the potential new man in my life. Neither Henry nor I seemed to know what to talk about, so we said very little to one another. As close as Henry and I were, I never thought that would happen. Zoe did her best to keep the conversation moving along, but she was struggling to make it work.

I said nothing during the meal and was thankful that we left as soon as we were done. I could feel the eyes of every patron stare at us as we walked out of the country club and headed to his truck. Vivian and her sisters left while we were eating, saving me from having to decide whether to introduce her to Colin there or leave it for a different time.

"So," I said, finally breaking the silence after we pulled out of the parking lot, "was there anything about that lunch that wasn't awkward? If so, then I missed it."

The guys had ridden together so Zoe and I would have a moment alone to talk. She wanted all the details of our date. But the couple was riding back together, and Colin was driving me back to my car in front of Zoe's shop.

"I'm sorry. Henry and I shouldn' have elbowed our way into your lunch. It seemed like a good idea when he and I had breakfast at the diner."

"It's okay. How was breakfast, anyway?"

"Enlightenin'."

"Care to elaborate?"

"Maybe on our next date."

"Was this a date?" I asked sheepishly.

"I would say yes. A double date." His smile grew as he answered.

"Okay."

I didn't know what else to say, so I let the silence fill the truck's cab. Colin pulled up behind my RAV4, parked on the street, and killed the engine. We both unclicked our seatbelts.

He turned to me. "Is this still weird for you?"

"Yes, but less weird than yesterday."

He smiled. "Good."

Colin cupped my chin with his hand, tilting my head to his. When I looked into his piercing blue eyes, I saw something I missed the night before.

Desire.

He leaned in until our lips were an inch apart. "I'm goin' to kiss you now 'less you stop me."

When he said those words, all I could think about was his sexy mouth on mine. The thought made my heart race.

I said nothing.

A moment later, his lips were on mine. His kiss was firm and commanding. My stomach flipped in response.

He knew what he wanted and wasn't afraid to go for it. Placing his free hand behind my head with a firm grip, he pulled my face tight to his and slid the other hand down my body, grazing my neck and the outer edge of my breast until he gripped my waist. He continued the kiss when he heard "Mmm" escape my mouth, and I felt my moan vibrate along his throat as I rested my hand on it.

We continued for a couple of minutes before he ended the kiss. He shook his head in shock and surprise as he spoke.

"Jesus, Cass, that was hot."

No one had ever called me Cass before. I liked the way it sounded, coming out of Colin's mouth, with his heavy Irish accent.

"Uh-huh," I replied in a daze.

I thought Edward had kissed me in every way it was possible to be kissed. I was wrong. Colin's kiss left my head spinning. It was the first time I had experienced any romantic physical contact in three years. I had no idea how much my body craved it until his lips met mine. It only took a moment before I thought of all the things I wanted to do with him and all the places where I wanted him to kiss me.

"I should probably go so you can get back to work."

"I'll text you about our next date," he said.

"Okay."

I hopped out of his truck and watched as he drove away. I was unlocking my car door when I got a text from Zoe.

Zoe: Holy Mother of God! That was one hell of a kiss!

Were you spying on us?

Zoe: Yep.

I sent her a smiley face emoji and then started the engine.

Twenty minutes later, my phone rang.

"Please stop making out with my brewmaster on Main Street in the middle of the day! God, Mom! I have never been so embarrassed in my entire life!" Hope hung up.

I considered the best way to handle it and realized that, after some thought, I should probably warn Colin, so I texted him.

Warning: Hope is on a tirade.

Colin: I heard her yelling at you.
I was the person who hung up the phone.
Things got heated after that. So, I walked out of the building.
I'm getting some coffee & letting her cool off.
I won't make many demands of your daughters.
But they will be respectful of you when I'm around.

I'm so sorry.
You did not sign up for this.

Colin: No worries, my beauty.
You're worth it.

I thought that would be the end of the comments, but I was wrong. I had decided to walk through the fields, as it was the first day the wind wasn't biting cold and the sun was shining. I was at the outer edge of the wine field when my phone rang.

"You've got to be kidding me," Brian said loudly into the phone. "After our conversation this morning, you have the nerve to behave like you did at lunch?"

"Brian, back it up. What are you talking about?"

"I heard that you were all snuggled up to him at the country club and then people saw you making out on Main Street."

"I was not snuggled up to him at the country club, and one kiss does not constitute making out." Although it was an awfully hot kiss, Brian didn't need to know that. "You know how the gossip is in this town. Take what you hear and cut it in half."

"Still don't like this guy for you."

Brian didn't wait for me to respond before he hung up. When he did, my mood flipped like a switch. He had the nerve to behave like this after we'd been friends for so many years.

Six

THE FOLLOWING DAY, I woke up early. Like most nights, I had not slept well, waking every couple of hours. I never remembered my dreams. I wasn't even certain I had them anymore, but the nightmares always stuck with me. And I had nightmares most nights.

I watched the sun break the horizon, got in my car, and was at the cemetery within minutes. When Edward first died, I went every morning as soon as I woke up. After six months, though, Vivian sat me down and gently ordered me to stop. She was right. It wasn't healthy. Soon after, I slowly cut down my visits to two or three times a month.

I pulled a blanket from the trunk to sit on but wrapped myself in it instead. February was always a cold month in Virginia. As I walked to his headstone, I thought about the February I spent in Australia and wished I were there again, enjoying the summer sun. I considered the possibility of traveling somewhere warmer next winter. When I reached Edward's grave, I sat on the frost-covered ground.

"Hey, honey." After a short second, I started crying.

I would give anything to hear him say "Hey, sweetie" one more time.

Leaning on the large marble stone, I pressed my forehead against it. I said nothing until the tears subsided. I had yet to visit his grave without crying at some point. Every time I visited the cemetery, I grieved everything I lost the day we buried his body. He was my friend, husband, lover, and father of my children. He was my everything.

"I know this is what you wanted, but I feel so guilty. Hope hates me right now. She was always your girl. The older she gets, the more I see you in her."

As usual, when I talked to Edward at the cemetery, I spoke in random thoughts with no connecting threads.

"Oh, guess what I found out? Faith has known about Tony for years. Alex accidentally said something but then swore her to secrecy. That girl is good at keeping secrets."

I sat for a while in silence with only a few birds chirping in the background.

"Edward, how do I do this? I know what you told me you wanted me to do, but . . ."

Deeply inhaling the morning air, I stopped talking and sat. I have no idea how much time I remained motionless, trying to meditate beyond my conflicted feelings and the guilt of going out with a man who wasn't him.

When I was done, I stood, kissed my fingertips, and then rested my hand on the top of his headstone, the same thing I had done to his casket after the funeral. It turned into a tradition.

I turned to walk back to my car in time to see Colin running along Cemetery Lane. During our dinner conversation, he told me he ran every third day. He ran daily when he was younger, but knee issues dictated a decline in the frequency of his runs.

After gathering the blanket, I walked to my car. I put it in the back.

By the time I closed the trunk, I was face-to-face with him.

He wiped the tears from my face with his thumb, holding his hand to my face longer than necessary. "He's buried here?"

I nodded.

"Will you show me?"

Colin's voice seemed exceptionally accented that morning.

I took his hand and silently made our way to the Baker family plot. Once we reached it, I dropped Colin's hand, kissed my fingertips again, and patted the top of Edward's stone.

Leaving Colin there, I walked back to my car. As I started the engine, I looked back to where Colin was standing. He was talking to Edward. I would never ask because I knew what the conversation was about. It was about me.

We didn't talk or text for the rest of the day. Or the next day.

However, on Sunday morning, I was sitting in my regular pew in church, the sun bursting in through the stained glass windows, making it difficult to see.

I was thinking about my girls and the changes in our lives over the last five years when I heard a familiar voice with an Irish accent whisper, "Is this seat taken?"

I slid over, and Colin sat next to me. I couldn't help but smile. Taking my hand in his, he returned the smile. I held it tight through the entire Mass.

After the service, he walked me to my car. I hadn't paid attention to what he was wearing when he sat next to me. I took a moment to appreciate that he was in dress pants, a shirt, and a tie. His long, gray, wool dress coat had enough material to cover my bed like a blanket.

"I'd invite you back for dinner, but Sunday dinner is one of the few things at Thomas Hall with rules. Family only. By order of the matriarch."

"I've heard a lot about Mrs. Vivian Baker."

"I think you'd like her. She already likes you."

Colin nodded as he opened the car door for me. "Maybe you and I can do dinner sometime this week? Your choice."

"I'd like that." He kissed my forehead after I sat, then closed the car door for me.

It was then I realized how much I truly liked Colin.

Later that evening, I found myself in the den of my house, drinking wine with Henry after dinner. I had talked to Zoe earlier that evening, requesting some time alone with him. I didn't have to tell her why. She knew.

Henry was nibbling at the charcuterie board the main house kitchen left in my refrigerator. I didn't think he enjoyed the mushroom ravioli, the evening's main course. Actually, I knew he didn't because he hated mushrooms.

"What do you think about Colin and me?"

My voice faltered, and I looked into my glass of wine.

He stared at me for a long minute before he responded. "You're struggling with this, aren't you?"

"Yeah, but I keep finding myself saying yes to him."

"I know I was quiet at lunch the other day. I thought I was completely cool with everything until I saw him hold your hand. I'm sure I'll get used to you being with someone that's not my brother eventually. But all of that being said, I think Colin is great for you. He's the kind of guy that could make you happy."

I nodded.

"Edward would want this for you."

I nodded again, hesitant to admit it to both Henry and myself. Because, if I could accept that Edward would want me to move on, I would need to define what my expectations were in a relationship. A relationship not with Edward.

"Sis?"

"I don't know if I can do this again."

My whisper was so low I was surprised he heard me.

"Colin understands how hard this is for you. We talked about it after your first date."

"Henry, he's a dozen years older than I am. You know what that means. Every time I think about it, I hear Darla's voice echoing in my head. 'Maybe you'll get a group rate at the funeral home for your husbands.'"

He sighed.

I knew he was remembering the snarky comment his first wife made when she learned Edward and I were engaged.

After a small silence, he looked at me and said, "If you could go back in time and choose to marry my brother, knowing exactly how it all would end, would you still do it?"

"Absolutely," I said without hesitation.

"But that's not really what this is about, is it?"

I shook my head. "I don't know how to do this. How do you define a relationship without the commitment of marriage?"

Henry leaned back in his chair and smiled at me. "You forget, Zoe and I have been committed to one another for over twenty years. We're both happy, and we never married. Commitment is love. Marriage is a contract. They don't have to go hand-in-hand."

I took a moment to drink my wine and contemplate what he said. "I guess so. I've always equated one with the other."

"I think, because you've had so few relationships, you failed to learn something important along the way."

"What's that, Dr. Phil?"

He laughed at my comment before he answered my question. When Edward and I first got involved, I had once caught Henry reading one of Dr. Phil's self-help books.

"Every relationship at each stage of your life is something different. So, you have to redefine love and what commitment should be each time. What worked in your twenties isn't going to work in your fifties."

My mind began to process what Henry was saying. He was right. I was starting a relationship differently from anything I had before. I was older, hopefully wiser, and had grown children to consider. I let a heavy sigh escape me before I spoke.

"I've got a lot to think about."

Seven

I STEPPED OUT OF the cold, rainy weather and into the brewery office on Monday morning with a box full of drinks from the town's only coffee shop, The Daily Drip. I sat a hot chocolate on the receptionist's desk, and on the way back, I placed various drinks on others.

Hope was on the phone, so I slid the mocha latte across her desk. She smiled back at me. At the next office, I knocked and then let myself in. Henry and Colin were sitting, talking about a scheduling issue.

I handed Henry his regular black coffee and then turned to Colin, handing him a flat white with an extra shot of espresso. I kissed his cheek and patted the top of his head as if he were a puppy dog.

A smile formed on his face as I took my chai latte out of the box, then left the empty container next to the trash can.

"How did you know this was my go-to drink?" Colin asked.

I gave him a mischievous smile. "Good question. Take a guess. Am I psychic, or did I bribe the barista?"

His grin was priceless.

"I'm going to go with bribin' the barista."

"Wrong."

"You're psychic?"

"No. The barista just told me. I didn't have to bribe her."

"I'm sorry. Who are you and what did you do with the very serious Cassandra Baker?"

Henry laughed.

Smiling, I shook my head as I walked toward the office door.

"Hey, sis, thanks for the coffee. Next time, though, you might want to wait for a response after you knock. What if Zoe and I had been in here having some alone time?"

"It wouldn't be the first time I walked in on the two of you."

Henry's face turned red. The incident was over twenty years ago, and it still embarrassed him. It still embarrassed me, too, but I had no problem using it as conversational ammo.

Colin stood and met me at the door. "I bet there's a story and a half there. Got a minute?"

"Sure. Maybe even two," I said with a smile.

"Henry, I'll be back in a few."

"Take your time."

I followed Colin into an empty office, and he closed the door behind us. He leaned toward me, brushing a stray wisp of hair away from my face.

One second later, my back was pressed against the door, and his lips were planted on mine. He was in complete control of our kiss and rapidly increased its intensity.

To balance myself, I pushed onto my toes, reached up, wrapped my arms around his neck, and gripped the hair on the nape of it. When I moaned into his mouth, he slowed the pace, as if we were treading into dangerous territory, which I think we were.

My imagination was running wild with possibilities. Possibilities I wasn't ready to act on but possibilities, nevertheless.

He pulled his lips away from mine when he said with a small smile, "I don' know what's goin' on with you today, but I like this flirty version of you."

"Henry gave me some things to think about yesterday. Things I had not even considered."

"Like what?"

"I'll tell you on our next date," I said, throwing his earlier comment back at him. "When is that, anyway?"

He was about to answer when the office intercom buzzed. "Mr. McAllister, the gentlemen from Whitmore Global Packaging are here for their appointment with you and Mr. Baker."

"Okay. Thanks. Take them to Henry's office. I'll be there in a minute." Colin looked at me. "I'll walk you out."

As we walked, he placed his hand on the small of my back. "Why don't you cook dinner for me tomorrow night in that fabulous kitchen of yours?"

Laughter poured from both Hope and Henry's offices.

"I'll be happy to have food brought in, but you need to know I can't cook."

"Of course you can. Everyone can cook somethin'."

Hope's head popped out of her office door. "Colin, after Dad died, we had to hire a chef to cook dinner every night."

"I flunked out of cooking school, too."

"I didn't know that, Mom."

I smiled.

When we reached the door, Colin leaned in for a kiss. I turned my head and gave him my cheek.

"Not in front of Hope," I whispered into his ear. "Not yet."

I was sitting at my desk, looking at Libby-Mae's new marketing campaign. It was brilliant.

Libby-Mae was my sister-in-law and the first person I hired after I took over the winery. I was about to email her when my phone pinged. It was Faith.

Faith: Did you really flunk out of cooking school?

Yep.

Faith: I thought you could do anything.

My mind flashed back to a day I couldn't do anything, the day Edward died. No matter how long I did CPR under the willow tree on that beautiful spring day, I couldn't save him.

My heart always hurt when I thought about that day. The anniversary of it was coming up soon, and the memory had been weighing heavy on my mind.

Faith: I'm coming home this weekend. Joy is too.
It's time you tell your daughters everything.
And we want to meet Colin before this gets too serious.

The five of us sat at the dinner table Saturday night, eating dessert, when I decided it was time.

I told them my whole life story as sleet beat hard against the windows. My girls knew bits and pieces of it, and Colin knew almost none. Everyone was social—everyone but Hope, who was silent and sullen.

I told them about my childhood, the death of my parents, and graduating from high school so young. My brother, Lewis. dying while I was in grad school, my subsequent nervous breakdown, and attempting to go to Le Cordon Bleu.

After dinner, we moved to the living room with a bottle of wine. Colin started a fire in the fireplace before I continued my story.

I talked about my marriage to Tony, the abuse, his organized crime family, and the faking of his death. I told stories from my travels after Tony's faked death and how I ended up in—and released from—a Chinese prison.

That brought us to the Thomas Hall chapters of my life. I intended to continue, but it was after midnight.

"I think I should leave the rest for another time."

We went through three bottles of wine after dinner, and I was certain I finished at least one of the bottles myself.

"Mom," Joy said. "We know the rest. You can save it for Colin."

"Actually, no, you don't. There are things your dad and I decided you didn't need to know until you were grown."

"Like what?" Hope snapped.

She was in no better of a mood than she was when the night began.

"Like my being kidnapped—"

"We know about that. Dad constantly reminded us," Joy said.

"What we didn't tell you was that it wasn't for money. It was with the intention of me being used as a black-market organ farm." Everyone's eyes grew large. "And then there was being trapped in a burning building by a man who wanted me dead, Uncle Henry's first wife trying to kill me, and watching everyone in an entourage I was part of getting picked off by a hitman. And that's just the tip of the iceberg."

"Yeah, we're so not done yet." Faith yawned. "We'll continue this in the morning."

The girls said their good-nights, and Colin helped me clean up the glasses and dishes from dinner.

"Cassandra, you've had a hell of a life. No wonder you have nightmares."

I froze. "How did you know?"

"It was one of the things Henry told me at breakfast after our first date. He told me his brother confided in him that you rarely slept peacefully. Henry figured that if our relationship evolved into sharin' a bed, I should know why you would probably never stay the night."

Looking down, I shook my head and bit my lower lip. Colin put an index finger under my chin and lifted it until our eyes met. His lips grazed mine.

"It's late. I should go."

"No. You've been drinking, and the weather is terrible. Stay in the guest room. You shouldn't be driving."

"Are the girls goin' to be okay with that?"

Joy yelled from the top of the staircase, "It's fine with us. Don't drink and drive. But stay out of our mother's bedroom! You two don't know each other well enough yet."

While Joy was serious, we both laughed.

Eight

WHILE I WAS MAKING myself a second cup of tea, Colin walked up behind me and wrapped his arms around me, pulling my back into his chest. I was expecting him as I heard the shower in the guest suite running earlier.

"Good mornin', my beauty."

"Mmm." Closing my eyes, I leaned my head back onto his chest, savoring the moment. "This is nice."

"Have you been up long?"

"A couple of hours."

"Cassandra, it's only seven. How long did you sleep? Four, five hours?"

"It's fine. I only woke up once in the middle of it. It was a good night."

He turned me around in his arms, and I was met with an unhappy face. He placed a hand on my cheek. "That's not a good night's sleep. Have you ever talked to a doctor about gettin' some medicine to help you rest?"

"I tried several different meds. It just made it impossible for me to wake myself from the nightmares. It's really not so bad. You get used to it." I leaned in and squeezed him tighter. "Coffee?"

"Sure." He looked at my mug. "Please don't tell me you hate coffee."

"I don't care for it. I'm a tea drinker. But I do know how to make coffee."

"Are you goin' to Mass today?"

"No. The girls will be heading back to school later, and I want to spend as much time with them as possible." I prepped and started the coffee maker. "I'll probably go on Wednesday morning. What about you?"

"No. I think I'll skip today as well. I thought I might make you four ladies pancakes this mornin' if you're interested."

I called in a list to the main house, and the kitchen sent everything Colin needed to make pancakes, bacon, and scrambled eggs.

The five of us sat at the table and ate, and everyone waited for me to continue my life story. I told them about arriving at Thomas Hall, reconnecting with the handsome stranger I met on a plane, how the girls' grandfather was murdered, and how I nearly died.

My girls knew that their father and I had a short courtship and engagement but had no clue about the things that happened during my first year at Thomas Hall.

When I told them about my first husband's return and my subsequent kidnapping, everyone looked at me in shock. By the time I got to the death of my surrogate grandfather, Poppy, and Edward's first heart attack, they begged me to stop.

"I'm sorry, Mom, but I can't take anymore right now," Faith said, having barely touched her food. "How did you not completely lose your mind?"

"Did I leave out the nervous breakdown I had during our engagement?" I asked.

"Yes," they all replied in unison.

Joy was still wide-eyed. "I have to tell you, when I got into bed last night, I was so mad at you for keeping so much of your life from us. Now that I've heard it all, though, I get why you chose not to tell us."

"I understand why you can't sleep without nightmares now, too," Faith said. "I asked Dad about it a couple of times, but he would never tell me. He would only say that you'd had an unusual life prior to our births, and the nightmares were the product of it."

I looked at the clock. It was already one in the afternoon, and we were all still in pajamas. All but Colin. He was in his clothes from the previous night.

"What time is everyone heading back to school?" I asked to change the subject.

Joy thought before answering. "I should get on the road within the hour. I've got an exam Monday that I need to study for."

"Same here," Faith said. "I've got a six-hour trip, and I would like to get back to school before it gets too late."

"I think I'm goin' to head out and give you ladies a little time alone." Colin smiled as we both stood. He walked over to me, gave me a hug, and then kissed my forehead. "Thanks for havin' me, Cass. Text me later?"

I nodded, and as he headed to the door, Hope spoke up for the first time since she came down for breakfast. "Colin, the three of us are going to walk you out."

The girls slipped on their shoes and coats left by the door and followed him out. I walked over to the window and watched. When they got to his truck, Colin leaned against it.

I didn't know what the girls were saying to him, but he stood there and let them speak their piece. They stayed outside for a solid ten minutes before Colin hugged Joy and Faith, but Hope declined. Then he got into his truck and drove away.

I walked into the kitchen and loaded the dishwasher in an effort to tidy up. The girls filed into the kitchen and stared at me.

"Well?" I asked.

"I like him," Faith commented. "He's like a giant teddy bear." She flashed me her father's Cheshire cat grin.

Even though Faith was a carbon copy of me, she had her father's smile. All of my girls did. I knew she would say no more on the subject. She was my quiet one.

"I've got to admit, I really wanted to hate the guy, but I can't. He's so nice and really honest, too," Joy said.

"What do you mean honest?"

"I asked him if he was looking to marry you?"

"Oh God, please tell me you're joking."

"I'm not, but I liked his answer. He said he didn't know yet. That the two of you were just getting to know each other, and he didn't even know if that was something you wanted. And then he said that what you wanted from this relationship was more important to him than anything. Mom, he wants to put you first." Joy paused. "If this is what you want, if he is what you want, we approve."

"Mom," Faith said. "When did people start calling you Cass?"

"People haven't. Just Colin. Only Colin."

"Well, okay, then."

Faith and Joy were satisfied with Colin, but I was acutely aware Hope was, once again, silent.

After the girls left, Hope and I finished cleaning up and got ready for the evening. It was Sunday night, and Vivian would expect the family for dinner.

I wore a cobalt-blue V-neck dress with black heels, and Hope was wearing her favorite above-the-knee forest-green dress.

Hope and I walked to the main house. The wind had a frigid bite to it, even with our full-length wool coats and gloves.

"You've been quiet this afternoon."

"Yep."

"You don't like Colin, do you?"

"Of course I like him. I hired him."

"But that's not the same as him dating your mother."

We were at the front door of the main house and let ourselves in. We stood in the foyer and continued the conversation.

"I have no problem with him. I just don't want you to date him."

"Him or anyone?"

"Colin isn't Dad!" Hope screamed.

This meltdown was inevitable. Edward's death wasn't easy on the girls, but to a certain extent, Hope was still in denial. She had shut down her emotions the day after her father died, becoming the stoic, strong oldest child. I wouldn't have survived if not for her. However, until that second, I didn't realize how painful Edward's death still was for Hope.

"He isn't Dad, and I don't want him to be! If you date Colin, you're going to forget about Dad. I hate this! I hate you!"

She sounded like a petulant twelve-year-old, and I half expected her to stomp a foot as well. Hope turned and ran out of the house, slamming into Sam, Henry and Zoe's son.

After Hope ran off, Henry looked at me. "Should someone go after her?"

"Probably, but I'm not the person for the job. She hates me right now."

"I'll go," Grace, Sam's twin sister, offered.

"No. She needs advice you don't have the experience for yet, thank God," Zoe said.

As she walked away, I thanked her and told her where to find Hope, even though she already knew. She would be at the willow tree. So, Zoe headed off in that direction.

That ancient tree meant something different for everyone in the family. For Hope, it was where she and her father had tea parties when she was young. For me, it was the place where I first knew, without question, I loved Edward and agreed to stay a little longer at Thomas Hall. A little longer became twenty-three years. And counting.

Nine

SOMEHOW, ZOE CONVINCED HOPE to return and join the family for dinner.

After a tense meal, Hope excused herself and headed home. I sat with Noah and Alex in the library, and we talked about what was going on at the winery and what to expect in the months to come. I was walking home when my phone pinged. It was Colin.

Colin: Is everything okay?

Sort of.
You've won over 2 of the 3 girls.

Colin: Hope's not liking this, is she?

No. She's not. She'll come around.
I just hope she doesn't give you more hassle at work.

Colin: Henry has already talked to her.

I was told you were asked,
"What are your intentions with my mother?"

Colin: I was.

Sorry.

Colin: Don't apologize.
They love you.
They only want what's best for you.

We took the relationship slowly—at least slowly for me. Going out a couple of nights a week and texting in between. Dinner, movies, bowling, museums, all the usual date stuff.

It differed from my past relationships. Edward and I only went on one proper date before we were engaged, and my first husband, Tony, and I met in college. We hung out more than anything, as we were both living on college kids' budgets.

Most date nights ended with me and Colin making out on the sofa at my house. Every time I thought he would propose we go further, he gently announced it was late and that he should head home.

Without me having to tell him, he knew I wasn't ready to jump into bed with him yet. Even if the thought had crossed my mind more than once.

I was continually shocked that he didn't give up and dump me for any of the beautiful, single women in town who were closer to his age and flirted with him whenever we went out.

However, he ignored them. He treated me as if I were the only woman in the room and never took his eyes off me to glance at anyone else.

Colin and Brian quickly grew to dislike one another. The mutual loathing began about two weeks after we started dating. After a matinee movie, Colin and I headed over to Lucky Shots, the place in town to drink, dance, shoot pool, and play darts.

I had been wanting to learn to play pool, and Colin offered to teach me.

We had only been there a minute before Brian walked over to us. I hadn't said too much to Colin about Brian's attitude toward him. I introduced the two.

"I'm glad you two finally met," I said, tense. "Why don't I go get everyone a drink?"

"No, Cass. I'll go get the drinks. Why don't you find a table for us?" He leaned in and gave me a quick kiss on the lips before turning to Brian. "What can I get you?"

"Whatever you're drinking is fine."

Brian waited until Colin was at the bar, and we snagged the last table before he said anything.

"He didn't even bother to ask you what you wanted. That's rude."

"He knows what I want, Brian. It's one of the reasons we're here."

"Right," he said suspiciously.

"Are you calling me a liar?"

Before he could answer, Colin returned with two glasses of whiskey and a margarita on the rocks for me. He sat next to me, moved his chair as close as possible, and wrapped an arm around me after placing the drinks on the table.

After the first sip, Brian looked at the brown liquid. "What is this?"

"Peated Irish Whiskey. Connemara to be precise," Colin replied. "Why?"

"It doesn't taste like whiskey should."

"Wait a second," I said. "Is that the same whiskey we were drinking at your place?"

"You have a good memory." Colin leaned in and kissed me yet again. His whiskey-flavored lips tasted yummy, but this was a message from him to Brian as he made a big show of it. "You liked it, didn't you?"

Nodding, I watched as Brian and Colin drank. The two men stared each other down as they drank. I knew Brian wasn't enjoying his drink. His expression told me what I needed to know. In addition, Brian liked his drinks on ice, and Colin had brought them neat.

Even though the bar had its normal level of noise between the people, music, and pool balls crashing into each other, the silence at our table was unnerving.

I looked around the bar, searching for an escape. The two were still glaring at one another when I noticed an empty pool table.

"Colin, a pool table has opened up, and you promised you'd teach me tonight," I said as I stood.

"I didn't know you wanted to learn. I could have taught you," Brian said.

"You should've offered, then. Your loss," Colin said with a smirk. He grabbed both of our drinks and stood, joining me.

"Come on, my beauty," Colin continued before looking down at Brian, who was still seated. "You'd think her best friend would take the time to find out what she likes and make it their business to get to know the new man in her life."

Colin walked off before Brian could respond. He looked at me. "I hate him."

"Well, it's a good thing you're not dating him, then. See you later, Brian."

He had spent the last two weeks plucking my nerves about not going out with him. As much as I loved my friend, I wasn't liking his attitude since Colin and I had become involved.

As the evening progressed, every time I looked around, Brian was staring me down. I spent a lot of time checking my surroundings at Lucky Shots. I had been abducted from there before Edward and I were married, and it was over a decade before I could step foot in the bar again.

Colin must have noticed Brian staring, too, and was smart about making certain Brian got an eyeful of what Colin wanted him to know. He went to great lengths to keep his hands on me and his body pressed against me as he "helped" me with my form.

What I thought Colin didn't know was that he fueled a fire that would last for years. However, he had done it on purpose to light that fire. I would later learn that the guys had crossed paths one morning a few days earlier at the coffee shop, and it was a tense meeting that ended with Brian telling Colin to fuck off.

Brian felt that Colin, with his tattoos and misspent youth, wasn't good enough for me.

Colin believed that Brian thought he was better than everyone else because he was the chief of police.

About a week after the evening at the bar, I had to put my foot down on Brian's attitude the day he wrote Colin a speeding ticket.

Ticket in hand, I stormed into Brian's office. "What the hell is this?"

Brian grinned. "Looks like a speeding ticket."

I threw the paper onto his desk but did not sit.

"Two miles over the legal limit?"

I knew an indignant tone filled my voice but didn't care.

"Speeding is speeding."

"That's not even outside the margin of error on your radar guns."

"How do you know that?"

"You told me when Hope got her first speeding ticket. So, here's what's going to happen. You're going to make a choice. You can make this ticket disappear, or you can talk to my attorney when he calls you to the stand. I'm sure the city will love it when the police department gets sued by the Baker family for harassment. So, what's it going to be?"

"You wouldn't do that," he said, trying not to laugh and failing.

I pulled my cell phone from my coat pocket and dialed. "Hi, it's Cassandra Baker. I am. I hope you're well, too. Is Zachary in the office and available by any chance? I—"

"Fine. I'll handle it," Brian said.

Zachary O'Keefe had been the Baker family's lawyer since before I arrived at Thomas Hall.

"Never mind, Mary. Thanks. Bye." I hung up and turned my attention solely to Brian. "I'm sick of this nonsense. Get yourself sorted. I've needed my best friend lately, and you're falling down on the job."

"Maybe I don't want to be friends." He stood, pleading his case. "Maybe I want more."

"I told you over twenty years ago that we would never be more than friends, and that hasn't changed. One thing has become crystal clear to me today, though. You only want me when I belong to someone else."

He didn't say a word. When I reached the door, I turned back to him.

"You know I'm right," I said before turning and walking out of his office.

This was not the first time I walked away from Brian's office, angry with him. Somehow, though, this seemed different. More concrete.

I thought that Brian would quickly get over my dating someone besides him and our relationship would fall back into our comfortable best-friend groove. But he didn't.

The longer I dated Colin, the further apart we drifted. Even though I needed a guy friend to be a sounding board in helping me navigate a "normal" relationship. Somehow, I knew, though, he would never be that person for me.

Thank God for Libby-Mae. She and I spent many lunch hours sitting in my office, eating sandwiches, discussing relationships and dating.

It was wonderful to have someone to talk with about these things. I really didn't have any contemporaries. All of my friends and most of my family were either decades older or younger than me. Libby-Mae and I were only seven years apart. I felt like she understood what was going on in my life better than anyone else I could confide in.

Ten

W E SAT IN COLIN'S apartment once *Lawrence of Arabia* ended, which we had found on one of the streaming services. The only light was from the television. He drank a beer while I had wine. I knew what needed to be said.

"You told me on our first date that one of your regrets was not convincing the mother of your children to marry you. How important is marriage to you?"

"Why?"

I sighed. I had a feeling the words about to come out of my mouth would hurt him. I just didn't know what the extent of it would be. The way he looked when he talked about the mother of his children not wanting to marry left me with the distinct impression that matrimony was important to him. And I didn't want to deceive him into believing it was an option with me, either.

"Before we take this relationship any further, there's something we need to talk about. I don't plan on ever marrying again."

"Oh."

Silence.

It hung in the air for several minutes.

As we sat, I studied his expression. Disappointment laced the sadness in his eyes. He slouched into the sofa and then rested his forearms on his legs, hanging his head.

"Maybe I should go." I stood to leave, but Colin looked up and stopped me.

"No, don't go. I appreciate you being honest with me. I just thought that gettin' married would be somethin' I would do in my lifetime. Can I ask why you won't even consider it?"

"If I tell you, I'll only hurt your feelings more than I already have tonight and probably change your opinion of me." I made my way to the door. "I think it's better for both of us if I just leave."

In a flash, he was standing next to me and wrapping his hands around my waist.

"Tell me," he whispered, his Irish accent heavier.

As he spoke, he slid his hands onto my back and engulfed me in a hug. I took a second to enjoy him holding me. When I told him the truth, we would be done. I would miss his arms around me, but I had to be honest with him and myself.

"I won't marry again because I've already married the love of my life, and I know I'll never be able to love anyone else like that again. It wouldn't be fair to you."

I expected him to release me from his grasp and let me walk out the door. I wasn't prepared for what he was about to say as he pulled me closer.

"You don' think I already figured out that Edward was your soulmate? I knew that before we met. Hope's stories alone made that clear. I just want to be with you." He pushed a stray piece of hair out of my face and tucked it behind my ear. "Share our lives together. Yes, marriage is somethin' I want, but it's not a deal-breaker for me. Missin' out on everything you bring to my world, that would be a tragedy."

I looked into his beautiful eyes. He looked happy. I wished he didn't.

"You deserve so much more than I'll ever be able to give you," I said in a voice barely above a whisper.

He leaned down until our foreheads touched. "Is that why you've looked so sad all night? You think I'm settlin'?"

I nodded. "I know you are."

"Cassandra, you're somethin' brilliant and beautiful that I never expected to find in my lifetime. Anythin' you give to me is enough. I just want to be with you. As long as we are committed, I can easily live without marriage."

I remembered what Henry said about commitment equaling love, and that was the moment I knew I would have a man in my life again—for what I hoped would be a long time. A handsome, tattooed walking wall with an Irish accent and an understanding heart.

He leaned down to me until our mouths met. Within a second, Colin picked me up, and I wrapped my legs around his waist and my arms around his neck.

After a minute, he pulled his lips from mine but kept his head close.

"Cass, love," he let out a deep breath before he continued. "Tell me what you want tonight. I haven' pushed for more, but God, I want you."

I knew this conversation was coming. We had been seeing each other for a little over two months. I bit my bottom lip before answering.

"I want you, too. But I need you to understand something. This isn't going to be easy for me at first."

My eyes welled up with tears. I loved Colin, but I had been *in* love with Edward for over twenty years. I spent a lot of time over the last couple of months trying to come to terms with it all.

"I know. It's why I've never pushed."

"Maybe it's time you did." I watched his response with a small smile.

He carried me down the hall into his bedroom, placed me on the bed, and sat next to me.

"Cass, I should probably ask you something before we go further since you're still young enough. You said you had health issues after your youngest was born."

"I can't have any more children. I had an emergency hysterectomy after Joy was born."

"I would have loved to have children with you, but I'm probably a bit old for that anyway."

"Regardless of what you think, I know I'm too old for that." I smiled as I slipped my shoes off, letting them fall beside the bed, then stretched out across his giant mattress, which took up most of the room.

He followed my lead and, within seconds, was next to me on his side.

His fingertips grazed my neck and cheek, and he gently kissed me, aware of my nervousness.

"Relax. You're a bundle of tight muscles and knots. There's no rush. We have all night," he said. The moonlight from the window silhouetted his broad frame and chiseled face. "Roll onto your stomach, and I'll give you a back rub."

I was slow to follow his directions, so he picked me up and flipped me over. I laughed before his strong hands found their way under my sweater, and he worked through several knots that plagued my muscles. My sweater bunched up to my armpits, so I pulled it over my head. He moved his hands to my neck and took his time, relaxing every muscle, before his lips created a trail down my spine. He unhooked my bra when he came to it before continuing toward my waist. Sporadically, I shivered as his beard tickled my skin.

When his lips reached my jeans, he rolled me onto my back, and I let the bra slip away.

He hovered over me, so I grabbed the bottom of his shirt and pulled it over his head. For a man his age—of any age—he had a spectacular body. He was broad-shouldered and muscular, with well-defined abs and strong arms. The skin of his torso was covered in a large, tattooed scene that spilled over his shoulders and onto his biceps. I knew there was a story to it, but I would have to wait until later to hear it.

I instinctively traced the upper edge of this work of art with my fingernail. It was only then a smile found his lips.

"You are such a beauty, Cass." The heat of a blush filled my face. "You blush so easily, too. I love that about you."

Colin paused, and I knew what he would say next. I just wasn't sure what reply would instinctively fall from my lips.

"I love everything about you," he said.

"Colin, it's okay to say it. I love you, too."

His lips crashed into mine while I was still stunned by what I said. The words *I love you* never came easy for me. I didn't say it as often as I should to the people I loved. So, for that phrase to flow from my mouth so effortlessly was somewhat shocking. I didn't know if I was trying to convince Colin it was okay to say the words or if I was trying to convince myself.

It wasn't long before we were naked and under the covers. I never thought being with anyone but Edward would feel right.

But this did.

It was comfortable, demanding, and different from anything I experienced in the last twenty-plus years. Not better. Not worse. Just different.

"Are you okay?" Colin asked afterward as he gently cradled me in his arms. "I didn' mean to be so rough. I just couldn' control myself."

"You weren't that rough. It was different, though. I liked it."

He was more demanding in bed than any man I had ever been with. While there had only been two other men, they always gently nudged or guided me to where they wanted my body to be.

Colin physically picked me up and moved me around until I was exactly where he wanted me, doing whatever he wanted in the process. It was one of the hottest things I had ever experienced.

"What do you mean different?"

"You really want me to talk about that being different with you than with someone else?"

He knew I meant Edward, but there was no way I would ever say his name when I was in bed with Colin.

"I want to make sure you're happy."

"Did you not notice?" I asked with a smile. "You made me pretty happy. A few times, in fact."

He chuckled and pulled me closer to him, adjusting our position by sliding an arm under my neck and wrapping his other arm around my body.

"You have an amazing figure for a woman with three grown children."

"I'd argue that point, but I'm too relaxed. I can barely keep my eyes open."

"Then, sleep a while, rúnsearc." *My beloved.*

"It's late. I should probably head home soon, mo ghrá." *My love.*

"You speak Irish Gaeilge?" he asked in astonishment.

"Not fluently, but I know a little Gaelic." I smiled as I tried to escape his bed and made it as far as sitting up before he stopped me by using his arm to hook my waist. His warm, wet lips left kisses along the small of my back.

"Stay the night," he said between kisses as he worked his way up my spine.

"I'm not sure you're ready for my nightmares yet."

He gently tugged me until I put my head back on the pillow. He joined me, and I looked into his sapphire eyes. "Let's try and see what happens."

"Mmm, I don't know," I said. He snuggled closer into me to tempt me, and it worked. "But your bed is so comfortable."

His body shook when he chuckled.

"I'll be right back."

He was only gone a moment before he returned with both of our cell phones previously discarded on the coffee table and an extra charger. He plugged the charger in on my side of the bed and put my phone on it, then slid between the sheets with me after plugging in his.

He turned off the lights, and I picked up my phone. "I'm going to text Hope. I always make her text me if she's not coming home. I guess I should do the same."

I dropped her a quick message that I would not be home until morning and then turned my phone to airplane mode.

"Why did you turn your phone to airplane mode?"

"Because as soon as Hope gets that message, she'll text me, her sisters, and probably Zoe. I don't want my phone keeping you up all night." I put it away and snuggled up to Colin. "Good night."

"Good night, mo áilleacht." *My beauty.*

Eleven

THE NEXT TIME I opened my eyes, the sun was blasting through the window, and Colin was not beside me, but a note was.

Cass,
Had to go to work.
I know you usually don't go into the office on Fridays,
so I let you sleep.
Call me when you wake, mo ghrá.
Colin

I picked up my phone, and my mouth dropped open when I looked at the time. It was nearly eleven. I had slept for twelve hours.

I didn't have nightmares but a wonderful dream instead. It was unheard of for me to remember my dreams. For over two decades, I would wake most nights, having relived a traumatic event in my life. When I broke down and finally saw a therapist after Edward died, I was diagnosed with PTSD. I had tried many techniques and medications over the years, but nothing helped. Most nights, I would wake two or three times, often getting no more than five hours of sleep.

In my beautiful dream, my late husband came to me, smiling. Edward looked as he did when we met. He was in his forties, strong, handsome, smart, and full of life.

In those last months before Edward died, he was still handsome and smart. The other attributes had been stolen from him by time and a weak heart.

Edward and I sat on a black sand beach in Santorini at sunset. We were barefoot and dressed in white. His pants were rolled up to his calves, his long sleeves pushed up to his elbows. My white cotton dress flowed in the breeze.

His arms were wrapped tightly around me.

"Hey, sweetie," he said with a smile.

"Hey, honey. How are we here?" I ran my fingers through his thick dark hair, stopping at the nape of his neck.

"You tell me. It's your dream. You picked the place."

"I miss you so much."

"I know. And I know you'll always love me. But you're happy with Colin. I want that for you. He's a good guy. I like him."

"Me too."

"You more than like him. You love him."

I looked away, but he placed his index finger under my chin and guided my eyes to his.

"I'm sorry."

"Why? Just because you love him doesn't mean you love me less. Remember what we used to tell the girls? Love's not a puddle that can dry out but an endless fountain."

I continued to stare deep into his cocoa-colored eyes. I missed those eyes. He leaned in and kissed me. It wasn't long or intense. It was slow, sweet, and serene.

"Thank you for understanding."

"It's time for me to go," Edward gently stated as he stood, and I scrambled to my feet.

"Please stay! Or I could go with you." I grasped his hand, and tears streamed down my face.

"Oh, sweetie, you're a smart girl. You know that's not the way this works. It's not your time yet, and it won't be for a very long while."

"Will I see you again before it's my time?"

"I don't know. Even the afterlife is full of mysteries." He gave me one of his mischievous Cheshire cat grins. "Now, close your eyes so I can kiss you once more."

I did as he said, and he gave me one last kiss.

When I opened my eyes, he was gone. So were the beach and the sunset. My dream had faded into nothingness.

When I turned airplane mode off on my phone, the notification chime went crazy. People left texts all night long. Faith, Joy, Zoe, and, of course, Hope.

Reading them all, I chose not to respond to them until I reached the final text. It was from Hope.

Hope: I think it's time for me to move
into a place of my own. It's overdue.
And even if it wasn't, I can't stay in the house
Dad built for you if Colin is sleeping in your bed.

I had to say something. I wasn't sure if it was the right thing to say, but no other response seemed appropriate.

I'm sorry you feel that way about Colin.
I'll miss you but maybe it's time.
You're 22 and need your own space.

After I hit send, I called Colin.

"Sorry I didn't call sooner. I just woke up."

"Just now? I'll have to start callin' you my Sleeping Beauty."

"I don't remember the last time I slept so long. And so peacefully, too."

"Cass, love," he said, lowering his voice and sounding serious. "You didn' sleep peacefully. I woke up to you cryin' and mumblin' in your sleep. There was somewhere you wanted to go, but whomever you were with wouldn' let you."

"I'm sorry," I said, hating that I woke him.

Eventually, I would tell him about the dream, but it wasn't the right time. No man wants to hear you had dreamt of another man after the first night you shared a bed.

"It really was the best sleep I've had in a long while."

"Okay," he said. I could tell he wanted to argue the point but decided against it. "Lunch?"

"Sure. I need to get ready for the day and run a couple of errands. Why don't I come to the brewery when I'm done, and we'll go from there?"

"Sounds perfect."

Once we disconnected, I sent Zoe a text.

Are you at the shop? I need help.

Zoe: Of course. What's wrong?

Slept at Colin's last night.
Going to lunch in a bit.
Don't have a change of clothes or a hair dryer.

Zoe: Slept AT Colin's or WITH Colin?

None of your business.

Zoe: Girl! Get a shower.
Put on whatever you wore last night.
Come to the shop.
I'll hook you up.
And I want details!

Ninety minutes later, I was leaving Zoe's Boutique, hair freshly blown out, light makeup applied, freshly polished fingernails and toenails. I had on a cute pale green-and-cream knitted plaid skirt and cream top. I thought my black flats were fine, but Zoe insisted on changing them out for open-toe cream sandals. It was still a little cool for sandals, but as usual, she was right. Everything looked perfect.

When I walked into The Baker's Dozen Brewing Company, I went to see Hope before I caught up with Colin. Her office door was open, and I watched from the doorway as she read a report. She looked the most like her father. Faith was the most like me, and Joy was a carbon copy of Vivian.

Hope ran her hand through her hair, just like Edward did when he was flustered.

"Does something have you rattled?" I asked.

Hope looked up. I think she wanted to be mad at me but couldn't find it in her.

"So many things, Mom. I put an offer in on a high-rise in Tokyo last week."

"Working on your own business today, then?"

"Yeah, I might be in over my head, too."

I sat down across from her. "Well, I'm sure there's someone we know that can help you. Do you want me to ask around?"

"Not yet. I want to try to do this myself." She paused and looked at what I was wearing. "Cute outfit."

"Thanks." I hesitated before I continued. "Are we good?"

"Yeah. We're both right, too. It's time for me to move out. I've been thinking about it for a while, and I think now, since your relationship with Colin seems to be evolving, it's the right time. The guy living on the third floor of the apartment building across the street from here is moving out at the end of the month. I own the building, so I think I'm going to take it. I'll have it painted, updated, and the floors refinished before I move in, though. So, it will probably be a few months before I'm gone from Thomas Hall. My question is, are you all right with it?"

"Hope, I adore you, my child. But you can't live your life around me. Live your own life. I'll be fine. I'm making a new life for myself, too. You know you're always welcome in my home, but it's time for us both to be on our own."

"The text I got last night makes me think you won't be alone."

"Probably not. Are you ever going to be okay with that?"

"I don't know, Mom. But it is what it is, and I know Colin will treat you right."

I stood and smiled. As I did, Hope walked around her desk and gave me a hug.

After, I went downstairs, heading toward Colin's office. It wasn't a bottling day, making it easy to hear voices coming from it. When I entered, Colin and Henry were sitting, having a beer.

"Isn't it a little early for that?" I asked.

Colin put down what looked like an empty bottle on his desk and made his way to me, smiling. He wrapped me in his arms and pressed his beer-flavored mouth against mine, reacting as though we'd been apart for months, not hours. Neither of us let up on the kiss until Henry cleared his throat.

"Do you two need some privacy?"

Colin ignored him and focused his attention on me. "You look beautiful. You went back to Thomas Hall?"

"No, Zoe dressed me at the shop." He smiled, and I leaned into him. "Lunch?"

"Absolutely."

Henry joined our conversation.

"Lunch or a trip back to Colin's place?"

"Lunch." I rolled my eyes and smiled. "Want to join us?"

"Where are y'all going?"

I looked to Colin for an answer.

"Anywhere Sleeping Beauty wants is fine by me."

"Did you just call her Sleeping Beauty?" Henry asked, amused.

"I slept for twelve hours last night."

Henry looked at Colin and back to me, astonished. "Damn."

I knew what Henry was thinking and felt my face get hot.

Colin saw my red face and steered the conversation back to lunch. "Where to, beautiful?"

"Pizza by Elizabeths?"

The guys nodded, and we headed out the door. For a moment, I thought about inviting Hope, but I knew she would be miserable eating with me and Colin. I texted her that we were going and offered to bring her something back, but she replied that she had been to lunch there the day before and was going out with her cousins, Sam and Grace, for an early dinner at the Mexican restaurant.

When we opened the door, the bright springtime sun blinded us. It was a glorious spring day. Not too hot. Not too cold. Henry rang Zoe as we walked to see if she had time to join us. She said she would meet us there shortly and told us her order. And as we made our way down the sidewalk to the restaurant, Colin wrapped an arm around me and kissed the top of my head. Life was good.

Twelve

I LOOKED OUT THE window as soon as I opened my eyes. It was mostly dark as the summer sun began to lighten the night sky. It had been months since I had woken this early. Rolling over, I found Colin's piercing blue eyes staring at me. It was strange to see him there. We had shared many nights over the last six months, but this was the first time we were waking in my bed.

When Hope was still living at home, the meltdown of having him spend the night wasn't worth the trouble, so we stayed at his place. But she had moved into her own apartment the day before, and I missed sleeping in my own bed.

"Mornin', my beauty."

"Were you watching me sleep?"

"I love watching you sleep." He cupped my cheek in his hand. "Especially on nights like last night. You didn't have any night-mares."

"I never have them when I sleep next to you." He raised an eyebrow, and I knew what he was referencing—the first night we slept together.

He would never believe my dream wasn't a nightmare because I cried.

"Okay, almost never."

I could tell something was on Colin's mind. At first, I decided to wait until he was ready to tell me, but I grew impatient.

"What are you thinking about?" I asked.

"I want to talk to you about somethin', but I don't know how you'll react."

"Well, talk to me and find out."

"I know you've told me that you'll never remarry. But how would you feel about us movin' in together?"

I had thought about it, too. We spent more nights than not sleeping next to one another. It almost seemed silly to maintain two residences.

"When does your lease end?" I asked.

"Not until December."

"When do you need to let the leasing office know if you want to renew your contract or leave?"

"No later than October thirty-first. Either way, I don' think I'll stay there. It's too far away from everything."

When Colin first moved to Virginia after taking the job at The Baker's Dozen, he rented an apartment in the next town over, in the opposite direction from Thomas Hall. From my home to his place was about a thirty-minute drive.

"At this point, I guess I just want to know if we should be lookin' together or if I'm on my own."

Closing my eyes, I inhaled deeply. I didn't know how he would react to what I was about to suggest.

"What if you didn't look at all?" I asked.

"Sorry, I'm not followin' you."

I swallowed hard before I spoke, but my voice only came out as a whisper. "What if you moved in here?"

He didn't respond but stared at me.

"I know I would need to change out all of the pictures and empty some closets, but if I did, would you consider it?"

"If I do this, I wouldn't want you to change a thing that you don't want to. Closet space would be nice, though." Colin grinned and kissed my forehead.

Although it had been a few years, I never emptied Edward's closet and dresser after he died. I tried several times, only to end up a blubbering, crying mess for days. Instead, I put everything of his in the closet or drawers where it belonged and closed the door to his dressing room.

"No, if you do this, you deserve not to see dozens of photos of my late husband."

"Whatever you want to do is fine. To be honest, I hadn' considered moving here a possibility."

"Why?"

"The girls. Specifically, Hope. And how would Miss Vivian feel about me living at Thomas Hall?"

"Vivian's been asking me for months when you would be moving in. As for the girls, they are grown and gone. Although, I highly suspect Faith will return to the nest after graduation. But she adores you."

"You should talk to Faith before she graduates and make sure it's okay. If not, we could look somewhere else."

"Colin, I can't explain it to you, but I can't leave Thomas Hall. When I arrived for Crush Weekend twenty-three years ago, I never left. I couldn't then, and I can't now. This place is a magnet for me. If you want us to live together, it has to be here."

"So, does that mean you'll let me move in?"

A wave of panic flowed over me, so I wrapped my arms around him and pulled myself tight against him before I answered.

"Yes? I think."

He chuckled at my uncertainty but had the perfect solution. "Why don't we do a test run? Maybe the month of October. After Crush is over at the winery. I can bring some things, and we'll see how it goes."

The tension that built in my shoulders during the conversation began to subside, and I nodded.

We would see how it went.

Deep inside me, I already knew it was a done deal. By the time the holidays rolled around, I wouldn't be looking at an empty pillow every morning—at least for what I hoped would be a long while.

Want to see more of Cassandra and Colin? You'll find them in The Baker Legacy Series, coming in 2024.

Also By Beth Sorensen

Welcome to The Oyster Bar: a story of love & death

<u>The Thomas Hall Series</u>
Crush at Thomas Hall
Divorcing a Dead Man
Waiting for Time to Tell

About the Author

Beth Sorensen, a Virginia native, graduated from Old Dominion University with an undergraduate degree in Geography. She spent most of her childhood summers on the Northern Neck of Virginia, where her novels take place.

Beth is a cancer survivor, mother of three, and currently lives in rural North Carolina with her husband. She enjoys good wine, great food, and a quiet beach.

She is the author of *The Thomas Hall Series* as well as *Welcome to The Oyster Bar: a story of love & death*.

www.bethsoren.com

Acknowledgements

When I sat down to write the the first novel of my new series, The Baker Legacy Series, coming 2024, nothing happened. The ideas were there, but the characters wouldn't show up and tell me what to say. So, I went back to the character I knew best, Cassandra Baker. One night, I decided to do a simple writing prompt: Where would Cassandra be once her children were grown? My response would go on to become the first draft of *If I Can Do This Again.*

In addition to my fictional muse, as always, there are many people to thank.

Stefanie Lewis, you are my alpha reader, bestie, top contributor. None of this would exist without your support. Thank you for everything. (And bite me!)

And, of course, my beta readers are incredible. Including my alpha reader, they are four women from four parts of the country, with four unique perspectives on reading, life, and love. Dezi

Webler, Jen Laning, and Kathy Hawkins, thank you for taking the time out of your busy lives to provide feedback on my work.

And finally, the list would not be complete without my editor and proofreader, Samantha Pico of Miss Eloquent Edits. I am a better writer because of you. Thank you!